BOOK 3

Nugget's
Dog Park Adventure

BY **Molly Wigand**   ILLUSTRATED BY **Sandy Koeser**

Hallmark
GIFT BOOKS

It was Monday morning, and Nugget was ready for another day at Doggy School! After giving his kids slobbery doggy hugs, Nugget jumped out of the car and ran into his classroom.

All his dog friends were already there, and Nugget was super-duper happy.

Today all the dogs were on their leashes.

"Do you know where we are going?" Nugget asked Victoria.

She had a mischievous smile. "Yes, but you'll have to wait and see. It's a surprise!"

The dogs trotted out the door on their leashes. They walked, and they walked, and they walked.

There were so many new things to see! And every time he saw something new, Nugget took a great big sniff.

Before long, the dogs arrived at the biggest grassy place Nugget had ever seen.

When they got inside the fence, the teachers let the dogs off their leashes. Nugget's friends ran in every direction.

They were free to run and play in the park, and Nugget couldn't wait to explore.

Nugget quickly dashed away.

Soon Nugget came across a puffy gray tail. "Hey, puppy!" said a squirrel. "Bet you can't catch me!"

Nugget laughed. "Bet I can!"

Nugget and Squirrel played tag until Squirrel scampered up a tree.

Nugget jumped up high, but he couldn't reach.

"Oh well!" he thought. There were still so many other things to see in the park. "See you later, Squirrel!"

He heard some distant quacking sounds, and this made Nugget a little curious.

Nugget saw three baby ducks following their mother.

"Hello, little doggy!" said the smallest duck. "Want to play follow-the-leader?"

Nugget joined the duck parade. He followed the ducks over a hill and toward a small lake, where they started swimming.

"Aren't you coming?" asked Nugget's tiny duck friend.

Nugget shook his head. "No, thanks. I don't know how to swim yet."

So the ducks quacked goodbye, and Nugget quickly dashed away.

Nugget stopped when he spotted a robin hopping on a picnic table.

"Hi, puppy!" said Robin. "You really should hop up here. The last picnickers left bread crumbs!"

Nugget tried to get on the table. It was tough, but he finally made it.

"Good job!" said Robin. "It must be hard not being able to fly."

Nugget licked up some crumbs. "It's okay," he said.

He had made a bunch of new friends today, and Nugget was super-duper happy.

Eventually Robin had to get back to her nest, so Nugget flopped in the grass and smiled. Then he looked around.

"Where are my school friends? I don't see them anywhere," he thought.

He looked at the hills around him, but they all looked the same. He started walking in one direction, and every few steps, Nugget took a great big sniff.

But Nugget couldn't smell anyone! There wasn't even a hint of Hugo, Victoria, or Pickle.

Suddenly Nugget grew a tiny bit worried. "Am I lost?" he wondered.

Nugget roamed the grassy space. Soon he passed Robin again, sitting up in her nest.

"Do you remember which way I came from?" he asked.

Robin looked down. "I think so," she said. "Follow me."

As Robin took off in the sky, Nugget ran behind her.

Robin and Nugget found the parade of ducks.

"It's my duck friends!" Nugget cried. "Can you tell me which hill we crossed to get here?"

The mother duck pointed to a flower-covered hill and said, "It was that one. Actually, I think I just heard some barking over there."

Nugget's tail wagged. That was great news!

"Oh, thank you!" he said. And Nugget quickly dashed away.

Nugget sped over the hill. There were his friends, barking up Squirrel's tree!

The dogs stopped barking when they saw Nugget running toward them.

Nugget was so glad to see Hugo, Victoria, and Pickle. His friends were totally terrific!

"Where have you been?" Victoria asked Nugget.

"Over there," Nugget explained. "I found new friends, and then I lost my old friends!"

Hugo smiled. "Well, I'm glad your new friends helped you find your way back to us!"

"Me, too," sighed Nugget. As he nuzzled his dog friends, Nugget was super-duper happy.

Pretty soon, it was time to go back to Doggy School. The walk back made Nugget's legs very tired. He had a busy day!

So it was no surprise that when he got back to school, Nugget settled down for a nice doggy nap.

Nugget awoke as his kids ran through the door. "We heard you went to the Dog Park!" they said. "Did you have a good time?"

"Ruff! Ruff!" Nugget replied. He was trying to explain that it was also a Squirrel Park and a Duck Park and a Robin Park.

They piled into the car, and Nugget cuddled up next to his kids. It felt great. Because Nugget loved his family more than anyone could imagine.

If you've loved reading this story with Nugget,
say, "I love you, Nugget."

Please send your comments to:

Hallmark Book Feedback

P.O. Box 419034

Mail Drop 215

Kansas City, MO 64141

Or e-mail us at:

booknotes@hallmark.com